W9-BSR-247
WITHDRAWN

DOROTHEA LANGE
LIFE THROUGH THE CAMERA

About the WOMEN OF OUR TIME™ Series

Today more than ever, children need role models whose lives can give them the inspiration and guidance to cope with a changing world. *WOMEN OF OUR TIME,* a series of biographies focusing on the lives of twentieth-century women, is the first such series designed specifically for the 7–11 age group. International in scope, these biographies cover a wide range of personalities—from historical figures to today's headliners—in such diverse fields as politics, the arts and sciences, athletics, and entertainment. Outstanding authors and illustrators present their subjects in a vividly anecdotal style, emphasizing the childhood and youth of each woman. More than a history lesson, the *WOMEN OF OUR TIME* books offer carefully documented life stories that will inform, entertain, and inspire the young people of our time.

Also in the WOMEN OF OUR TIME Series

BABE DIDRIKSON: Athlete of the Century
by R. R. Knudson

ELEANOR ROOSEVELT: First Lady of the World
by Doris Faber

DIANA ROSS: Star Supreme
by James Haskins

John San Francisco, California, 1931

DOROTHEA LANGE

LIFE THROUGH THE CAMERA

BY MILTON MELTZER

Illustrations by Donna Diamond
Photographs by Dorothea Lange

VIKING KESTREL

For Janie, with love

M.M.

VIKING KESTREL
Viking Penguin Inc., 40 West 23rd Street, New York, New York 10010, U.S.A.
Penguin Books Ltd, Harmondsworth, Middlesex, England
Penguin Books Australia Ltd, Ringwood, Victoria, Australia
Penguin Books Canada Limited, 2801 John Street, Markham, Ontario, Canada L3R 1B4
Penguin Books (N.Z.) Ltd, 182–190 Wairau Road, Auckland 10, New Zealand

First published in 1985 by Viking Penguin Inc.
Published simultaneously in Canada

"Women of Our Time" is a trademark of Viking Penguin Inc.

Library of Congress Cataloging in Publication Data
Meltzer, Milton, Dorothea Lange : life through the camera. (Women of our time)
Summary: A biography emphasizing the early years of Dorothea Lange, whose photographs of migrant workers and rural poverty helped bring about important social reforms.
1. Lange, Dorothea—Juvenile literature. 2. Photographers—United States—Biography—Juvenile literature.
[1. Lange, Dorothea. 2. Photographers] I. Diamond, Donna, ill. II. Lange, Dorothea, ill. III. Title. IV. Series.
TR140.L3M443 1985 770'.92'4 [B] [92] 84-13124 ISBN 0-670-28047-X

Printed in U.S.A. by The Book Press
1 2 3 4 5 98 88 87 86 85
Set in Garamond No. 3

CONTENTS

1

"I Watched"

They called it "thieves' highway." After school Dorothea had to walk the shabby length of the Bowery for nearly a mile on her way to the ferry crossing the Hudson River. On every corner were petty thieves selling the goods they had stolen. Block after block, Dorothea stepped across the bodies of drunks sprawled on the sidewalk. She was twelve years old then, and scared, but she knew how to show no feeling so she would draw no attention.

She would use that expressionless face her whole life in making photographs of people in strange places.

"I can turn it off and on," she said once. "If I don't want anybody to see me, I can make the kind of face so no one will look at me." It was hard, walking the Bowery twice a week when her mother was working the night shift. But it helped prepare her for the work she would later give her life to.

Dorothea lived across the Hudson in Hoboken, New Jersey. Her mother, Joan, had a librarian's job in New York City on the Lower East Side of Manhattan. Every day she took Dorothea to a school near her library. Dorothea was the only non-Jew in that ghetto school. She felt like an outsider. She thought she was bright, but she found it hard to keep up with kids so hungry to learn, so eager to fight their way up out of the slums.

After school, Dorothea would sit in her mother's library, waiting to go home with her. The library windows looked out on noisy streets full of peddlers and pushcarts. Hundreds of thousands of immigrants were packed into the most crowded district in New York. Dorothea could look straight into the life of the brick tenements. She could see parents, grandparents, children, boarders—talking, cooking, sewing clothing in kitchens used as workrooms. "I looked into all those lives so strange to me," she said. "I watched."

She acted like a camera. Her intense look focused on details. The hands of the choirmaster conducting in church. A bunch of lilacs resting in a passenger's lap on the ferryboat. The multicolored washline in her backyard tracing a vivid pattern against the late-afternoon sky.

She spent endless hours looking at photographs. She studied them in the library, on the walls of her classroom, in the newspapers and magazines she clipped and saved at home. All kinds of pictures interested her. She pinned on her bedroom wall the best she could find.

She was unhappy in school. Nobody seemed to know who she was, or care. She had few friends. Dorothea didn't join clubs or play games. She liked best to sit in her mother's library and read. Or watch people through the windows.

Dorothea's grandparents on both sides had moved from Germany to America, hoping for a better life. They settled in Hoboken. Her father was Henry Nutzhorn, a young lawyer. He married Joan Lange, the librarian. Dorothea was born on May 25, 1895. The family lived on the first floor of a new brownstone house they rented on Bloomfield Street. The neighborhood was block after block of row houses bordered by trees. Dorothea's was a restless family; they moved several times from one New Jersey town to another, then back to Hoboken.

At seven, Dorothea came down with polio, a paralyzing illness. This was long before there was a vaccine to prevent people from catching it. The disease damaged Dorothea's right leg, from the knee down. It made her lame for the rest of her life.

The other children called her "Limpy." It hurt her feelings. Even her mother sometimes acted as though she were ashamed of her crippled child. When Dorothea was out walking with her, and some friend came along, her mother would whisper, "Now walk as well as you can!" Why did her mother care so much about how she looked? It made Dorothea bitter. She could never forget her handicap. But it did not make her withdraw from the challenges of life.

Dorothea's mother was a handsome woman—strong nose and mouth, freckles, rosy skin. She wore her chestnut hair in the style of that time, with a big knot on top. She enjoyed the taste, touch, and smell of things. She spent what she could of her small earnings on books and records. She liked to talk about what was going on in the world, and when she saw people treated unfairly, she tried to do something about it. Dorothea loved her very much. Still, there were things about her mother she didn't like. Joan was too fearful at times, especially of what the neighbors might say.

Dorothea loved her father, too. At home he had a

great big book of Shakespeare's plays. Dorothea read the tiny print till she was dizzy. She didn't know or care that it was poetry—it was the stories she was hungry for. Her father would laugh and quiz her to see what she knew about this play or that. One day, when she was ten, he took her to see a performance of *A Midsummer Night's Dream.* He hired a coach and horse, and they drove to the theater in style. But there were no seats left when they got there. Her father wasn't upset. He stood in the back and lifted Dorothea on his shoulders so she could see the play over the heads of the crowd. It was a magical evening.

And then, one day, he left her. It happened when she was twelve. The marriage of her mother and father broke up. Her father deserted the family. She never saw him again. He did not visit, or call, or write, or even send her mother money to help support the family. Why he went away was a mystery to Dorothea. It was so terrible a blow that she almost never mentioned her father again.

When Dorothea was graduated from P.S. 62, she went uptown to Wadleigh High School. The school was flooded with girls—3,600 of them!—and its huge size made her miserable. It was too strict for a girl who loved her freedom. She often skipped classes, walking from above 100th Street way downtown to the Battery. She liked roving these crowded streets, soaking up impressions of city life. She wanted to reach out and bring everything close to her.

Her mother didn't know how often she was on the loose. Dorothea didn't mind that. She was glad her mother was too busy trying to make a living to watch over her every minute.

Dorothea was not a top student in high school. She did best in the arts but the school did not think they were important. If a student failed just one course the school flunked her out. She would have failed physics if her teacher hadn't upgraded her final exam so she could graduate. Dorothea learned from her what being generous meant. That teacher, Martha Bruere, was a plain-looking woman who dressed plainly, too. Like all the other women teachers, she was not married. She cared a lot about science and social issues. She became Dorothea's first adult friend. Miss Bruere's father was a surgeon, her brother a leader in reform politics, and her sister, against great odds, had become an executive in a big bank. Dorothea was very proud of that family—so different from her own—and pretended that they were her real family.

Dorothea's grandmother Sophie Lange, a tiny woman, lived with them. She was a widow and made her living as a dressmaker, a very talented one. Once she told Dorothea that of all the beautiful things in the world nothing was finer than an orange. Look at it, she said, see how perfect it is just as a thing in itself! Dorothea watched her cook meals. She did it in a careful, particular way. A dish had to taste just right: she threw it out if it wasn't just right.

But Grandma Sophie had a terrible temper. In a family quarrel she would say threateningly, "You hear me not saying anything?" When company she didn't like came to visit, she would suddenly call out, "Let's go to bed so the people can go home!" By the time Dorothea was in high school Grandma Sophie had become a messy old woman who drank too much and quarreled with Dorothea all the time. She hit the girl whenever she lost her temper. Dorothea's mother was too timid to stop her.

Great-aunt Caroline, a sister of Sophie's, also lived with the family. She worked in the public schools for thirty-five years, teaching the seventh grade, and never married. Caroline was the only one who could hold Sophie in line. Dorothea felt that Caroline was the reliable center of the family. She was a warm woman with a round face, a sweet smile, and strong opinions. Her students adored her. They could tell the coming of the seasons by Caroline's change of hats. She owned only two, one for spring and the other for winter. Grandma Sophie made her a new dress now and then, but Caroline hated to give up an old one, wearing it until the black turned green and shiny.

When Dorothea had a birthday, Caroline would always give her a crisp new dollar bill, fresh from the bank.

Still, even with Aunt Caroline for comfort, Dorothea stayed at home as little as possible and was out of school as much as possible. One classmate would be her lifelong friend. Their friendship started when Dorothea saw Florence pass in the hall and liked the way she swished her starched petticoat. Fronsie—her nickname—joined Dorothea in skipping classes, roaming in Central Park, going to plays and art shows and the Museum of Natural History.

Even with a friend, Dorothea thought of herself as a loner, a "lost kid." She taught herself, she would say, learning from everything, full of curiosity. When graduation time came, her mother asked, "What will you do now? What are you able to do?"

Dorothea knew.

"I want to be a photographer," she said.

2

Apprentice

A photographer?

When she had no camera and had never taken a picture?

Dorothea's decision was a great surprise to her mother. Joan could not believe her seventeen-year-old daughter would ever make a living at it. Work for women in the early 1900s was very limited. A factory hand, a nurse, a teacher, a librarian, a secretary. Photographers? Who knew any women who did that? Joan insisted Dorothea must go on with school and prepare to be a teacher. That was a sure thing. So Dorothea went to a teacher-training school in New York.

Her heart was not in her studies. She went to classes but thought about how to learn photography. She had always loved pictures, all kinds of pictures. Now she wanted to make her own pictures. True, she had never owned a camera, but she knew that was what she wanted to do, *must* do.

Which master would she learn from? She started at the top, but quite by chance. Walking on Fifth Avenue one day, she noticed some portrait photographs in a display case at street level. They were the work of Arnold Genthe. She went upstairs and asked him for a job. He was one of America's great photographers. He was famous for his pictures of the San Francisco earthquake of 1906. And many famous people had sat for his portraits—presidents, actors, writers, opera singers.

Why did Genthe take on this raw beginner? Surely there were plenty of young people eager to work for little money in such a place. She must have made a blazing impression on him. Not because she was beautiful, or even pretty. She wasn't. But she was an attractive young woman, with a freckled, fine-boned face and eyes of greenish blue, more green than blue. He hired her at once, then said, "I wish you'd take those red beads off. They're not any good." She decided he was right, and she never wore cheap jewelry again.

Genthe's studio gave her a look into a world of wealth and celebrity she had never seen. Her days took on a new pattern. Every morning she crossed by ferry from New Jersey to Manhattan to reach her first class at 8:40. And when school was out at 3:00, she hurried downtown to learn the craft she was committed to. It was a remarkable thing for a seventeen-year-old to do.

She worked in Genthe's studio every afternoon and often into the evening. She learned from his two assistants how to take his negatives and print proofs from them, how to use a brush to retouch negatives so spots wouldn't show, and how to mount and frame the finished photographs. From Genthe himself she learned something else. She saw that he appreciated women and understood them. He could focus on the plainest woman and his picture would show the light he found inside her. He was a real artist, she thought. He made pictures that went below the surface. He showed the true character of the sitter. Here was someone who did what he wanted to do, and loved it.

Teacher-training school seemed a waste of time now. Dorothea dropped out and her mother had to accept it. To get more experience, Dorothea left Genthe and spent six months at another studio. There she learned how to run a portrait studio as a business. She began by using the telephone to line up customers. She learned all the tricks of the trade: what customers wanted and what they didn't want, how to please them and how much to bill them.

But she still did not know how to make pictures with the big camera the professionals used. So she moved to another studio, run by a woman who hired camera operators. Dorothea watched them closely as they worked. One day a portrait commission from the wealthy Brokaw family came in. But no one was on hand to shoot the pictures. Desperate, the woman asked Dorothea to do it.

"It was the first big job I ever did," Dorothea said. "I was scared to death I wouldn't be able to do acceptable pictures." But she took the big 8 x 10 camera out alone, and did it. She had learned how professionals behaved on the job and what people wanted from a studio portrait.

The results pleased the Brokaws and her boss. Her next job was to photograph a famous British actor, Sir Herbert Beerbohm Tree. She was nervous and uncertain. But he liked her and gave her confidence. It made the job easy. She became the studio's official camerawoman.

There would be four or five other photographers she would learn from in one way or another. They were lovable old hacks, she thought, not artists. But they liked her eagerness, and patiently answered her technical questions. She found out how important it was to have a good negative. Other things she learned in reverse—what not to do. She was a sponge soaking up whatever seemed useful. One wandering old photographer came to her New Jersey home with samples of his work under his arm. She learned he had no darkroom, and said he could use the old chicken coop in back. She worked with him to rebuild it into a darkroom, learning how it was done and what equipment was needed.

Now she had her own "studio." She was bringing home money to help support the family. She was showing she could be independent. Her mother stopped nagging her. "My daughter's a photographer," she proudly told the neighbors.

Dorothea smiled when she heard that. Yes, but with a lot to learn. She had a big camera and two lenses. Night and day she worked at improving her technique. Photography is "a gambler's game," she said. Unless you work to a formula, the result is never a sure thing. You have to take chances. She enjoyed the process of making something. With your eyes, your hands, your heart, your imagination, you shaped something. And when you were finished, there it was, a real thing.

In 1917, when she was twenty-two, she signed up for a professional course with a master photographer, Clarence White. He had a fine sense of the human figure and what light could do playing over it. He used the camera as a natural instrument, the way a musician plays the flute. He was the rare kind of teacher who did not lecture. He gave her a nudge here, a nudge there, to encourage her on her own path. He had an uncanny gift for touching the lives of his students.

That year Dorothea made many portraits on her own—of family, friends, neighbors, children. All without pay, just to try it out, to learn what she could in her chicken coop studio. Men began to appear in her life. One was a sculptor, another a printer. And both much older than she. She thought the sculptor was slightly crazy. He would suddenly appear at her home, without calling, at all hours. And sometimes he was drunk when he came. He was the first "real" artist she had met. Were they all like that? And then there was the printer. He was a hard worker who made her the center of his life for two years. He sent her letters three times a day. He wrote her poetry, bought her records, took her out to elegant dinners. But nothing came of it.

By 1918, when Dorothea was twenty-three, she and her friend Fronsie "just knew" they had to get away from home. Dorothea thought she could earn a living with her camera wherever she chose to go. And Fronsie was a Western Union clerk whose company said she could work in a Western Union office in any city. They decided to go around the world. Dorothea's mother thought it a wild idea and hollered she'd never let her go. But they went, with about $140 in cash and one suitcase. When they got to San Francisco, they were robbed. To eat they had to find work. Dorothea landed a job making prints from the negatives customers brought into Marsh's, a camera supply store.

Stopping in San Francisco proved to be a dividing line between past and future. She threw away her father's name, Nutzhorn, and took her mother's name. Her life back home, her growing-up years, suddenly faded out. From now on she would be known to everyone as Dorothea Lange.

3

Troubled Years

Through Marsh's store Dorothea began to make friends, and to take photographs of them. She joined a camera club to get the use of its darkroom. There she made more friends. A year later a generous businessman helped her to open her own portrait studio.

It was in a handsome little building on Sutter Street. For years it would be the center of her life. In the late afternoon friends would drop in for tea and talk, or to dance to the new jazz recordings. In the basement Dorothea built a darkroom. She got her customers in the usual way. The satisfied ones told others how good she was. One wealthy woman liked the portraits she saw in the display case outside. She had Dorothea photograph her family. Their pleasure in the results made Dorothea the favorite photographer of the leaders of San Francisco.

She was soon busy enough to work day and night and weekends. She did not think of herself as an artist. She was simply a professional doing everything possible to make portraits as good as she could. She wanted to be honest and truthful in her work. She was trying to record on film human beings you could look at, and into.

One day in 1920, a friend brought a man named Maynard Dixon into the studio. And six months later, Dorothea married him. She was twenty-five, he was forty-five. Dixon was a painter of the western wilderness, its people, animals, and landscapes. He was a tall, lean, handsome man, with a sunburned face and piercing eyes. They loved each other. But as the years passed, it turned into a stormy marriage. Neither of them worked just to pay the bills. They worked for the sake of the work—because of an inner need. And they let their work cut painfully into their personal life. Dixon often went alone to other cities to paint murals, or into the mountains to paint Indian life. He would be gone a long time. He did it even after they had two sons, Daniel and John. Sometimes they boarded the boys with others when they thought their work demanded it. They felt bad, but they did it. It made the children very unhappy to be separated from their parents.

In these years a few art collectors began to buy photographs as well as paintings. Some of Dorothea's portraits were chosen. It was the first sign of recognition that she was an artist. Still, she gave Dixon's painting first place in their life. She did all the housekeeping and took care of the children.

Times were better when the whole family could go up into the Sierra Mountains for a vacation. The children loved those weeks. On these trips Dorothea began to use her camera on landscapes. But the results were bad. She wondered where her photography was going. One day, as she was sitting alone on a big rock, a roaring wind came up and a thunderstorm exploded around her head. She wrote later that suddenly "it came to me that what I had to do was to take pictures and concentrate upon people, only people, all kinds of people, people who paid me and people who didn't." She always remembered this as one of the great spiritual experiences of her life.

A few months later, in the fall of 1929, the stock market crashed and the Great Depression began. It was the worst economic disaster the country had ever

suffered. Businesses came to a dead stop. Around Dorothea, one friend and neighbor after another lost their jobs. The grocery on the corner closed, then a shoe store, a dress shop, a gas station. Salesmen in the big department stores were laid off. Factories stood silent, the smoke from their chimneys gone. Banks shut their doors. Within a year one out of every four workers was jobless.

With times so bad, even the rich stopped ordering photographs. They stopped buying paintings. Something terrible was happening. Because people didn't understand it, they felt panicky, lost. It was like being caught in the slowly closing jaws of a vise. Dorothea and Maynard found it hard to make ends meet. He sold a painting here, she a portrait there. But not many: these were luxuries few could afford.

One day Dorothea was standing at her studio window, staring down at the street below. She saw an unemployed young man drift by, stop, turn, look this way, then that. She wondered, Where can he go? What can he do? There was no planned welfare then. No program to put people back to work. Dorothea's portraits of the rich and comfortable were no longer real to her. It was on the street that real life was going on. She left the studio and went down into the streets to photograph.

Almost at once she saw how photography in a studio was very different from photography outside. Upstairs she could arrange her subjects. Now she had to train herself to select them, and to shoot at the decisive moment. It was scary, going up to strangers with a camera. Down the street she saw jobless men standing in a line, waiting for free food. A rich woman known as "The White Angel" had set up a place to feed the hungry. Dorothea turned her camera on the line, and made three shots. Why this subject? She didn't know. All she knew was that she wanted to be useful, to help them somehow.

It turned out to be a natural thing for her to do. On the first day she took what has become one of her best-known photographs, "White Angel Bread Line." It is one of the most moving images of what happened to Americans in the 1930s. It was art for life's sake.

She pinned the print to her wall. A customer looked at it, and said, "Yes, but what will you do with it?"

Dorothea had no idea. She simply had to respond with her camera to the life that beat in upon her. She made more and more pictures out on the streets. Seamen and longshoremen on the waterfront went on strike for better wages and working conditions. Dorothea's camera captured the bloody clash with the police. Her lens caught pictures of homeless families

White Angel Bread Line San Francisco, California, 1933

trudging the highways, of people evicted from their homes, of picket lines and protest meetings and hunger marches.

She had found her commitment—to people. At this moment in American life, it was to the people tossed on the garbage dump by a wrecked economic system. She remembered her childhood walks on New York's Bowery. Here, too, she herself was not one of the homeless and hungry. But she had to move with her camera among angry and bitter men and women. She was afraid at first, but she taught herself how to do it. She still had to make studio portraits to help support her family. More and more, however, she wanted to give her whole self to this new work.

An opening came when a new president, Franklin D. Roosevelt, took office in March 1933. He knew that after years of hunger the people wanted action. He had shown courage in overcoming the polio that had crippled him in both legs. He could understand human suffering and he was not afraid to experiment. First came federal funds to relieve the suffering. Then huge public works projects to provide jobs for the unemployed. The fog of hopelessness began to lift.

Dorothea soon got her chance. It happened when a photography gallery asked to exhibit her new work. "Documentary," they called these photographs. The

Latin root of that word is *docere,* to teach. Documentary photographs are important because of their power not only to inform us but to move us. Dorothea wanted her photographs to touch the viewer, to open heart and mind to the world we live in. Paul Taylor, a college professor in nearby Berkeley, saw her show and liked it. He borrowed her pictures for an article he wrote about the waterfront strike.

Soon he took Dorothea with him to visit a commune near San Francisco. It was one of the many self-help groups that sprang up as a way of meeting the problems of the unemployed. These people banded together to get through the Depression by doing work in exchange for the fruits and vegetables the local farmers could not sell. Dorothea watched Professor Taylor interview them. He drew facts and feelings from them so gently they did not realize how much they told him. She saw how eager most people are to talk, even to strangers. The more so when they talk about their own lives. Taylor in turn watched her make pictures of the same people. He liked how quietly she did it, and the meaningful details her camera caught.

Paul Taylor was an economist raised in Iowa. He had the prairie farmer's pride in his own land and labor. He wanted to use his knowledge to make people's lives better. He believed you could bring about

Depression San Francisco, California, 1934

change if you took the trouble to find out what was wrong and to think through what to do about it. His fine mind could get to the heart of a question, and organize the facts to win public support for making a change.

In Dorothea, Taylor saw a photographer with deep feeling for people in trouble. Her eye looked for the heart of a situation and the details that revealed it. Her pictures recorded both the life in front of her lens and her feelings about it. She always made pictures of people with respect for their dignity.

In the mean, cold winter of 1934–35 she saw strangers streaming into California. They came by the tens of thousands. They were farmers from the Midwest and Southwest, hit hard by the Depression. Great dust storms following a terrible drought had ruined vast tracts of farmland. The desperate farmers took to the roads, fleeing what was called the Dust Bowl. They joined the harvest hands and migrant workers. They followed the seasonal crops as pickers and laborers. If they earned a hundred dollars a year they were lucky.

The hungry men, women, and children wandered over California's rural counties. The state had few or no means to shelter and feed them. The government turned to Professor Taylor for help. Find out, they said, what the trouble is. Why so many migrants?

Children of Migrant Workers California, 1936

When will they stop coming? What can we do about it right now?

Taylor knew the Depression was only partly to blame. Another cause was the increasing use of new machines—tractors, mechanical pickers—to replace human labor. And a third force was such natural disasters as drought and dust storms. He agreed to find out how the state could help the migrant families.

Paul Taylor knew that the bare facts alone would not get politicians to act. Give them a mountain of statistics and they would yawn. They needed to *feel* what was wrong. So he hired Dorothea to make pictures of the terrible conditions the migrants lived in. "My words in reports won't be enough," he said. "The people who make decisions need to *see* what these lives are like."

They both knew that photographs of a social problem were quite rare. They had seen the pictures Jacob Riis had made in the 1890s of the New York slums, and Lewis Hine's heartbreaking images of children working in coal mines and cotton mills. But most scientists paid no attention to pictures. Research had to be "objective," they thought. Keep it cool. Leave out the feelings. Not Taylor, he didn't think that way.

Dorothea went on field trips with Taylor. She was the first to photograph the migrants. She and Taylor worked together, preparing reports strongly illustrated with dozens of her photographs. The soft-voiced, bright-eyed woman with the weather-beaten face and short-cut hair would walk up to the migrants and look around quietly. She wore slacks, and a beret cocked over one ear. Perhaps when they noticed her limp they knew she, too, had been hit by the unfairness of life. She would wait till they got used to her. Then she'd talk with them. When they seemed to accept her, she would start taking pictures. What made her good at it was her natural feeling for people. She could put them at ease, make them feel she cared. She never shoved her camera into anyone's privacy. If people did not want to be photographed, she would not find some sneaky way to do it. If she saw they were shy, or suspicious of a stranger, she would just sit in a corner and let them look her over. Then she would speak to them about who she was, what her family was like, why she was here. Always the truth. It took more time that way. But it was the human way to meet other humans.

4

Migrant Mother

What Paul Taylor and Dorothea worked on together made a difference. Taylor asked the state to set up camps where the migrants could live decently in tents or mobile homes. The government in Washington liked the idea. It gave California money to build the first of many camps. Then Dorothea shot pictures to show what the camps did for the migrants. Here are teachers working with preschool children, nurses caring for the sick, people cooking and washing and cleaning, men making music with fiddles, folks sitting around in the recreation hall, playing cards or just talking.

The Taylor-Lange reports were passed around Washington. The President's wife, Eleanor Roosevelt, saw them. So did senators and cabinet members. They saw more of her pictures of the poor in national magazines. Dorothea's pictures had a powerful effect. "It's a revelation, what this woman is doing," they said.

In the fall of 1935, a government agency concerned with farm problems hired Dorothea. Her new boss, Roy Stryker, told her to go right on recording migrant life in California. That year was a great dividing line for Dorothea. She turned forty. She found her special gift as an artist. And she ended one marriage and began another.

Dorothea's marriage to Maynard Dixon had long been in trouble. On a field trip with Paul Taylor—they were the same age—she realized she was in love with him. He was married, too, but had been unhappy for many years. They both obtained divorces, and they were married in December. They went to live in a redwood house on the side of a hill in Berkeley. It overlooked the campus of the University of California, where Paul taught. Around the house ran a garden Dorothea liked to work in. In the basement she built her studio and darkroom.

On her new job she often had to work in painful heat or cold, in storms of rain, sand, wind. The end of a

long workday was always a welcome relief. Yet at the moment she was doing her job, she felt happy and fulfilled.

In March 1936 she had been out alone on the road for a month. It was late winter, the weather still raw and miserable. It was raining as she drove north for home. Her camera bags were packed. The rolls of exposed film were safe on the seat beside her. She speeded along the highway, thinking of home.

Out of the corner of her eye she saw a sign flick by—PEA PICKERS CAMP. She didn't want to stop. She drove on. But she could not forget that sign. How were the pea pickers doing in that camp back there? Shouldn't she take a look? No, she had plenty of pictures on that subject. This would only be more of the same. And if she took her camera out in this rain, it might be ruined.

For twenty miles more she drove. And suddenly

she made a sharp U-turn on the empty highway. She went back those twenty miles to the sign, PEA PICKERS CAMP.

"I was following instinct, not reason," she recalled later. "I drove into that wet and soggy camp and parked my car like a homing pigeon.

"I saw and approached the hungry and desperate mother, as if drawn by a magnet. I do not remember how I explained my presence or my camera to her, but I do remember she asked me no questions." Dorothea made five exposures, working closer and closer to her subject. "I did not ask her name or her history. She told me her age, that she was thirty-two. She said they had been living on frozen vegetables from the surrounding fields, and birds that the children killed. She had just sold the tires from her car to buy food. There she sat in that lean-to tent with her children huddled around her, and seemed to know that my

Migrant Mother Nipomo, California, 1936

pictures might help her, and so she helped me. There was a sort of equality about it."

Dorothea could not have known it then, but on this field trip she made one of the great American photographs. Called "Migrant Mother," it has been seen countless times. In books, magazines, newspapers, pamphlets, films, television programs, and exhibits all over the world.

As soon as Dorothea got home, she developed the film and rushed the still-wet prints to a San Francisco newspaper editor. The pea pickers, 2,500 of them, she told him, are stranded by a crop failure. They're starving, and no one is paying attention. The paper reported the story, running her pictures with it. The federal government rushed in 20,000 pounds of food to feed the hungry migrants.

"Migrant Mother" is a work of art that has had its own life. Dorothea would become known everywhere for this image of mother and children. Yet her life with her own children and stepchildren was painful and troubling. In her new marriage with Paul there were five children to care for. Her sons were now ten and seven. Paul's children—Ross, Margot, and Katharine—were thirteen, ten, and six. They had come to live with him while their mother was in New York studying for a doctoral degree in clinical psychology so she could earn her own living.

Here were Dorothea and Paul—two professionals with full-time jobs. Often, both were away from home as a team. Or Dorothea went on the road alone. What to do about their children? Earlier, she had placed her boys in boarding schools or in someone's home. Now, when Paul and Dorothea went off on government projects for two or three months in the summer, they left the boys and girls with foster families.

It was bad for the children. And it cost Dorothea much to treat them this way. Here she was leaving her children behind, so she could take pictures of other mothers trying to take care of *their* children. Within a year or two she began to show the signs of an ulcer. She was torn between family and career. She never felt she met the full demands of either. She wanted to be perfect in all she did. And demanded that of the children, too. She was quick to get angry when they fell short of her expectations. Even holidays or trips planned for fun would turn sour because she lost her temper or was too bossy. She loved the children, yes. But she did not respect their right to be themselves. It was *her* tastes, *her* dreams they had to fulfill.

The five boys and girls never knew what mood she would be in. They were scared to do or say something that would bring on her anger. Paul's children had known lots of laughter in their first home. There was little in this one.

5

The Power of Pictures

In the summer of 1936, Dorothea took her first field trip in the South. She stopped in Washington, the nation's capital, to meet her boss, Roy Stryker. He was a big tough westerner, with a square face, glasses, and warm, sparkling eyes. He wanted his camera crew to make pictures that captured what was happening day by day. Show me, he said, how life is changing. Look for the details. Ask questions. Listen to people. Find out what they think. And bring me back the images that express what you learn.

Like Dorothea, Stryker cared most about ideas.

Skill with a camera? That was just the means to an end. To most of us, he would say, the world is a blur. The photographer's job is to pick out the meaningful things from it and make the rest of us see them and understand them.

Dorothea drove south in her old battered Ford. The drought was still cursing the land. Crop losses were enormous. Preachers conducted prayer meetings for rain. The topsoil blowing off in the wind darkened the skies. Uprooted tenant farmers rattled over the roads in their jalopies, heading for California.

Down through the Shenandoah Valley of Virginia she went. She watched farmers harvesting oats by hand, with a cradle scythe. They had never seen a combine harvester. She cut through Tennessee, her camera catching jobless men sitting on courthouse steps. In the mountains she saw tall, lean men looking like Abe Lincoln.

Across North Carolina she photographed poor whites swinging their hoes. In Birmingham she made pictures of workers in the steel mills. Out in the countryside, a black farm family told her they barely got by on $150 a year. It took the labor of all seven of them to earn it—mother, father, and five children. Peach pickers in Georgia said they earned only seventy-five cents a day. In the Delta region she made many pictures of the rickety cabins blacks lived in,

Hoe Culture Alabama, 1937

of their prayer meetings, of families walking home from church, carrying their shoes because they couldn't afford to wear them out.

The mean treatment of these farm people had begun long before the Depression. Without land, tools, or money of their own, they paid for the right to raise crops by giving 50 percent of whatever they grew to the landlords, who cheated them so they never got out of debt. Dorothea's pictures show trouble and sorrow she had once thought only famine or war could cause. They show whole families working in the fields from sunup to sundown. They show the sowbelly and meal on their tables. They show the sickness ruining their bodies. Nearly nine million people—half of them white, half of them black—lived like this in the South of that time.

As Dorothea moved along she sometimes mailed her negatives to Roy Stryker in Washington. Suddenly there was a great demand for such pictures. The press services, the newspapers, the magazines begged Stryker for photographs to illustrate their stories about rural poverty. Hers were often the ones chosen.

Near Oklahoma City, in sight of gleaming skyscrapers, Dorothea found people squatting in shacks with no sanitation. They hadn't worked for months, for years. In Texas she photographed some ex-slaves. In the 1930s there were thousands of them still living.

Her pictures show the cotton culture of south Texas—the hoeing, the picking, the weighing, the baling, the camps of the migrant workers. She crisscrossed the states on both sides of the Mississippi.

Late in August she was home again, with thousands of miles of travel behind her. Her first job was to develop the vast batch of negatives and send proof prints to Stryker. It was tough work for her. She knew what she wanted in a negative and print. The exposure—the shooting of the picture—was but the first step. Then came selecting the right paper and chemicals for the developing, drawing from the negative the rich range of tones that would make a beautifully detailed print. The developing work in the laboratory was not easy for Dorothea. She did not have a knack for it. She could have mastered the technical side. But her mind was fixed far more on what she was photographing and her feelings about that.

Once, long after these field trips, she took out a picture in order to make another print of it. She began telling the young man who was helping her in the darkroom of the time she had shot it, some thirty years before. And suddenly she started to cry. So many years had passed—and she could still feel the pain, the sorrow she had felt back then.

Those were the years when journalism took a new turn. Newspapers and magazines had used photographs for a long time. But mostly pictures of people in the news, of fires and floods and accidents and crimes. They had not sent out photographers to make picture stories of social issues. Now they could do it because of a new kind of camera. It was small, easily carried, had a fast lens, and used 35 mm film. It gave documentary photography a big push forward. Photographers had thirty-six chances on one roll of film. The little camera could make visual records easier and faster than the big old cameras.

The new camera became a tool for exploring those years of crisis. It showed Americans the truth about their lives. It made them know how unbalanced, how unfair, how wrong, how unjust their society had become. It recorded people at work, at play, at war, in the everyday round of life, in the cycle of seasons. It revealed how human beings behave, how they depend on one another. It recorded change: how cities grow or decay, how farming spreads or dies, how customs develop.

Dorothea often used the new 35 mm camera, but it was not her primary tool. She preferred larger cameras, choosing among them the best for the particular job facing her. She thought some photographers were more concerned with their craft than with their subject matter. For Dorothea, feelings about the power of images came first.

For four years Dorothea carried on her work in the field. She covered much of the vast American continent for Stryker's group. Their photographs were called "the most remarkable human documents ever rendered in pictures." They helped to change America. If life was made any better for the poor, Dorothea and her co-workers had much to do with it.

Their work showed the public the power of pictures. Millions of amateurs with camera in hand began to watch the world more closely.

6

The Right Time

In September 1939, Adolf Hitler, the German dictator, invaded Poland. The war everyone had feared began. World War II forced many changes upon the United States government, even though it had not yet declared itself at war. Projects like Dorothea's were cut back. Her job was taken away. She felt lost without it. She did not want to go back to studio work. Ever.

What to do now? She was granted a Guggenheim Fellowship—the first woman photographer to receive this highly prized award. She was to photograph the religious communities of the West, such as the Mormons in Utah. But on December 7, 1941, before she had finished the work, the Japanese bombed Pearl Harbor. Now the United States, too, was in the war. And the war gave her another project, suited to her genius. It happened this way.

The government made a hasty and tragic decision. It said it feared the Japanese Americans on the Pacific Coast would act as traitors and help Japan. So it forced all persons of Japanese ancestry to enter concentration camps. They sold their homes, businesses, and farms at great loss. Not one of the victims had done anything wrong. No one was ever tried in a courtroom. It was a ruling based solely on race prejudice. It wasn't done to other ethnic groups whose home countries were at war with the U.S. The Italian Americans and the German Americans were left alone. Was it because they were white? But Japanese-American men, women, and children, 110,000 of them, were put behind barbed wire.

Then the government did a strange thing. It decided to make a pictorial record of the roundup and internment, and hired Dorothea to do it. Today we see what the United States did as a terrible violation of human rights. It was like tearing up the Constitution and throwing it away. But back then most people did not see it that way. Only a few—and Paul Taylor was one of them—spoke up against the crime.

Internment of Japanese Americans Centerville, California, 1942

Dorothea hated the policy, too. This was a chance to show what its effects were. With her deep concern for human life and dignity, she went quietly about the job. Her pictures were buried in the files for thirty years. But in 1972 they were taken out and made the core of an exhibit shown in many museums around the country. She was the national eye of conscience. Her pictures remind us of the nightmare thousands of innocent people lived through as a result of racial hatred and wartime fears. They show another truth: that the Bill of Rights is not enough in itself. People must care enough to see that the laws are respected and enforced.

It was on this job that Dorothea began to feel bad pains from an ulcer. Still, she finished the work. Then she took on another government task. She made picture stories about ethnic groups on the West Coast. Their lives were being changed by the war. Many had taken jobs in the defense plants and shipyards. Her pictures were printed in United States magazines sent overseas. Airplanes scattered copies to the people in countries occupied by the Nazi army. The idea was to show how people lived in a free nation.

Dorothea's illness got worse. She had to have surgery. She went through three bad years before she could take up a camera again. Then slowly she began to make pictures, but they were different from before.

One series she called "relationships." Here is a family on the street, a father carrying his child, a couple holding hands, people eating in a coffee shop, a woman pushing a baby carriage, a gardener planting seeds.

This was everyday life. Gone were such powerful subjects as the Depression, the Dust Bowl, the war. Her focus was on the ordinary, the familiar, the usual. She could no longer go to where the big events were happening. She turned to the warmth and intimacy of human connections. "Things you have to look very hard to see," she said, "because they have been taken for granted not only by our eyes but, often, by our hearts as well."

There was more time now for her children and Paul's, and for the grandchildren. They had a simple wooden cabin on the California seashore. It had two small rooms, no electricity, no phone, no hot water. Weekends they drove up in their small Volkswagen with as many kids as they could gather. The children slept on cots or in sleeping bags. They used the cabin on weekends all the year round. It became the special place to be together. The three generations shared it and loved it. But Dorothea loved it perhaps most of all. For now she was knitting together a family that had known separation and great trouble.

They used kerosene lamps for light, the wood-burning stove for cooking, and the corner fireplace for heating. Dorothea prepared the meals. Paul took over the outside chores, and the children gathered the firewood and set the table. They went swimming or hiking, played games, read aloud their favorite books. There was music too, flute and clarinet.

At the beach Dorothea taught the children how to see in a way they hadn't learned to before. They would pick up pebbles and study them with her, waiting for a certain light, and she would take photographs of their hands holding pebbles, letting them see how different hands can look and how they move and how the changing light affects that look.

She always had her camera along. To them it was just a part of her, like her limp. Nor did she hide her sickness from them. Many foods she couldn't eat. And at night they could sometimes hear her labored breathing. Or her voice saying quietly, "Oh dear! Oh dear!" And they knew the pain was bad. But she took her illness so matter-of-factly it did not make the children feel sad.

She encouraged friendships among her grandchildren. They all grew up feeling close to one another. Once she told a five-year-old grandson that a cousin he was fond of couldn't come to his birthday party. And then she presented the little girl to him in a big gift-wrapped box. The holiday celebrations she planned for them were full of magic. The family was always there, with the circle widened to include friends and visitors. Sometimes as many as thirty-five sat down at their table. For each guest she chose a special present, each one wrapped differently. The family called her "the Napoleon of holidays."

Maybe she felt so strongly about tradition because her father had left the family, and because she had been too busy for them in earlier years. This was her way of making sure family ties would not be broken.

For a time Dorothea felt well enough to take on special jobs. With her friend Ansel Adams she did a story for *Life* magazine on the Mormons in Utah. He shot the landscapes and she did the people. Then *Life* sent her abroad, to make a picture story on the country people of Ireland.

For two terms Dorothea taught at the California School of Fine Arts. She gave her students what she had learned in a lifetime with a camera. Pictures too often show what things look like, she said, not what these things mean to the observer. She wanted the kind of picture people would look at and say not how did you do it, but *that such things could be!*

In the next few years Dorothea went abroad with Paul. He was invited by foreign nations to study their rural problems and give them his advice. He took Dorothea with him on three long trips. They went to Asia, later to Latin America, and finally to Egypt. While

Country Road County Clare, Ireland, 1954

working overseas under difficult conditions she suffered great physical pain from her ulcer. But still she produced some of her best photographs.

In 1964 the doctors discovered that she had a terminal cancer. "Just when I have gotten on the track," she said, "I find that I am going to die. There are so many things I have yet to do that it would take several lifetimes in which to do them all."

She asked her doctor to tell her the truth. How much time did she have left? From a few months to eighteen months, he said. What she did after that is hard to believe. Only a powerful will could have forced so ruined a body to go on until her work was done.

She prepared a photographic essay about the life of American country women. She took part in two television films about herself and her work. She developed a proposal for a national project on documentary photography. And, most important, she accepted the invitation of the Museum of Modern Art in New York to prepare a one-woman show of her life's work.

She kept doing her best to meet the needs of her family. Paul took over the household, the meals, her medication. She went over tens of thousands of negatives, before choosing the two hundred prints to go

on the museum's walls. Always she was in discomfort and sometimes in pain.

She took every day by itself. Each hour became precious. She did not think of the past. She wanted only to look ahead.

When her work on the exhibit was almost finished, a fever took hold. She was carried to the hospital. From her bed she sent messages to the museum about last-minute details. Then bleeding set in, and she slipped rapidly downhill.

Her family stood by her bedside. They had brought pine branches gathered in the hills. She smelled their fragrance and smiled. She whispered to Paul, "Isn't this a miracle, that it comes at the *right* time!" Then, soon after, "How fast it comes . . ."

She died on the morning of October 11, 1965. She was seventy years old.

Three months later, the exhibit opened at the Museum of Modern Art. "Truly great art such as Dorothea Lange's," wrote one critic, "belongs to all civilization." She was an artist, he said, who "discovers new truths in the cause of man."

ABOUT THIS BOOK

I wrote this biography of Dorothea Lange out of love and respect for a great woman. Not a "perfect" woman, for greatness in artists or scientists or political leaders does not come without the human weaknesses ordinary people share. I never met her, although I lived through the same Great Depression she knew. While Dorothea Lange was making photographs for one agency of the government, I was writing for another, the Federal Theatre. I saw her pictures then, and I keep seeing them again and again, for they are treasures of art and humanity that will always move those who look at them.

Some years ago I wrote a much longer book, called *Dorothea Lange: A Photographer's Life.* For it, I interviewed nearly one hundred people. They included Dorothea's family, friends, neighbors, and schoolmates, as well as photographers, editors, and writers who had known her. I thank them again for sharing with me their knowledge and impressions. I also thank the staffs at the Oakland Museum in California, the Museum of Modern Art in New York City, and the Library of Congress in Washington, D.C.

When I quote what Dorothea or others said, and when I write about thoughts she had, it is not made up. All of it comes from what was recorded in letters, diaries, and interviews.

Remember, this is how one person sees and tries to understand another person's life and work. The biographer's job is to try to get as close as possible to the complicated truth of another human being. M.M.